Buying this book or downloading it you donate 50 cents to the IHP association for the health and the safety of all the mistreated horses:

www.horseprotection.it

On their side

Humans don't always learn easily what respect for life is. They don't consider other animals as companions with which to cohabit, but like things to use and throw away afterwards. Horses, more than other species, suffer from this culture, which has little that is natural and a lot that is anthropocentric. A horse is hardly considered a friend, because he is always a horse “to do something”: trotting horse, racing horse, jumping horse, dressage horse, riding school horse, carriage horse, circus horse…slaughtering horse: the same terminology underlines that he doesn't exist as an individual in the average consideration, but only on his utility. He doesn't have rights. IHP was born to encourage a change and to shake consciences: it is our solemn commitment to equines, who make us better persons with their gentleness, their depth and their pride.

My blogs:

www.samilla.wordpress.com

www.catastinisamanta.ilcannocchiale.it

www.italianromances.wordpress.com

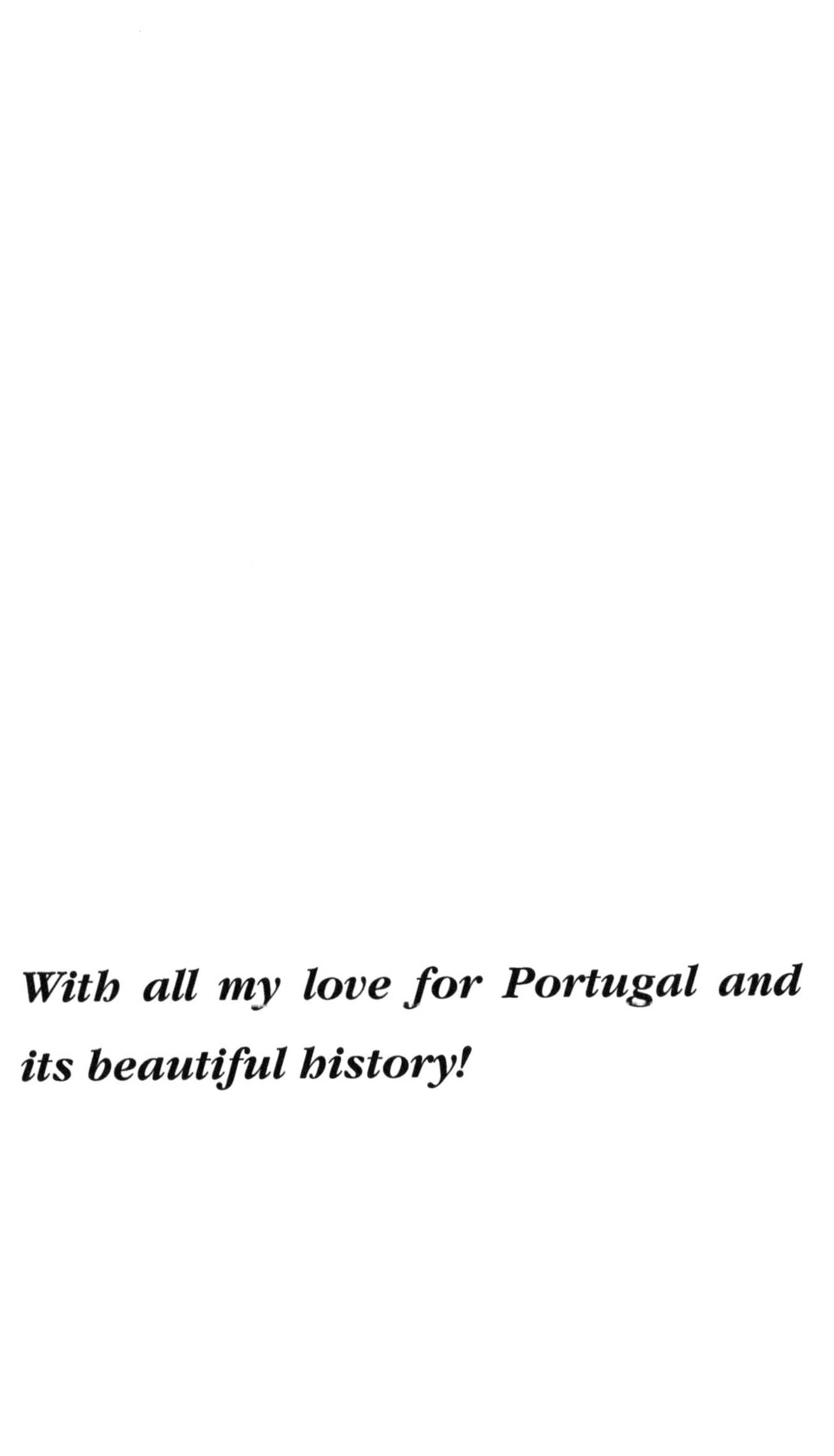

With all my love for Portugal and its beautiful history!

Samanta Catastini

LOVE'S HOPE

Translated by Cristina Contilli

The Marquis Pombal (1699-1782) Minister of the Kingdom, namely, head of the government during the reign of José I (1750/1777) is a person really existed. The other characters in this novel are fanciful.

Love imposed is as a cut flower. It withers even before it blooms... (Samanta)

Così per me tu reggi la vita e la morte racchiuse nella luce dei tuoi occhi, e sai darmi con il tuo sguardo morte e vita,

e io sono felice, anche se la mia sorte dipende da te;

se mi dai la morte, presa da te la morte mi sarà gradita.

Luís Vaz De Camões.

(Trad. dal portoghese Catastini Samanta)

I dedicate this book

to Cristina Contilli…

1756, Porto, Palacio do Freixo

1.

“Baroness Da Costa, where are you?" The shrill voice of Mary, her maid, resounded in the park of the palace Freixo. Doroteia tried a bit of calm in the gardens, while she was overlooking the River Douro. The flow of water, when it was quiet and slow, cradling her thoughts and soothed her wounds. "I'm here! Don’t be alarmed." The girl reached in haste. "Your father is looking for you. He came the Marquis Armando Silva and he want to see you soon as possible." This word was her recurrent concern and, try as entertainment in the beautiful house that she lived, she could not find peace. Her future husband was omnipresent, but her unwelcome. She had had no choice but to agree to a union already decided by the father. The marquis was so closely with the King José and she can't lose a marriage proposal so propitious. Her family was greatly improved their social position and his father had acquired a prominent place in the good graces of the sovereign. Many noblewomen Portuguese wanted to be in place, not just the title that was acquired but also because Mr. Armando was very beautiful. Initially she thought loved him then, knowing him better, she had felt misunderstood and alone. He told her expectations, dreams and interests, and he seemed to listen but then forgot everything. Eventually he decided to keep everything for themselves. So every day her sadness and her isolation grew constantly greater. Doroteia knew he was very nice but she did nothing to show off. She had long brown hair, dark complexion and big brown eyes that amber laid bare his soul. "Tell them to join them now!" Mary had looked away in a hurry to bring the news to Baron Da Costa before he lost patience for the long wait. Then he climbed the stairs of the plane large garden overlooking the Douro and headed towards the great door of the sumptuous palace Freixo. On the way he repeated that had to be happy for what fate had given her. A comfortable life in a charming place and a future rich husband and young. Other girls of her age, twenty-four years had gone in marriage to men much older than them. Fortunately, in the eyes of his father, the social position of the Marquis Silva had precedence over other suitors, older and more affluent. He had many estates throughout Portugal and in Brazil, which exported gold and precious stones. Decided to enter from the rear of the building, he had turned once more toward the river before crossing the great gate, which is accessed by a grand stone staircase. The Italian architect Nicholas Nasoni, famous in the city of Porto and Vila Nova de Gaia to his many works, he built a complex in the Italian Baroque style. The building was designed with four large quadrangular pyramid-shaped towers. The facades were completely white, but enriched with sandstone surround the windows with garlands of flowers, masks, medallions and badges of Tavora and

Noronha family, owners of the house. The balustrade on the top floor was decorated with fake stone vessels. The interior was so rich and sumptuous breath-taking. Everywhere one could see beautiful stucco and painted tiles, typical of Portuguese culture. The most famous hall of mirrors that was a nice imitation of Versailles. The simplicity certainly did not live those rooms. When he knocked on the door of his father Jose was the waiter over to receive them with a big bow. The marquis had risen to meet her. Tall, dark eyes and light brown hair did not pass unnoticed. Yet his heart had not the slightest sign of emotion. He had heard that when you meet the eyes of the loved one seemed to stop breathing. The same sonnets of Luis Vaz de Camões it were a test. Those poignant words showed how much love had to be fundamental to the life of every human being. "Here here. Finally we have made search everywhere. But where were you in?" Only one string of inane questions he had sent off my head. How could he, after attending the month, not to imagine where he might have fled?"

2.

"Senhor do we do with this barrel?" Get in the store and be careful not to break or the Marquis of Pombal will have no pity for you!" Rodrigo had just arrived from Britain to control his land holdings and production of then world's most famous wine, the Porto. He decided to buy a house at Vila Nova de Gaia to follow more closely his commerce. A native of Braga, his family was one of the oldest in the city, however, he had lived the last years in Lisbon to finish his legal studies. Despite his huge fortune, he was fascinated by the economic production of Porto and he had done everything to open his own company, the Fifth Barros. He had invested much money and a lot of energy just to see her dreams come true. The Marquis de Pombal, the most powerful man in Portugal, as Prime Minister of King José I, had supported him and he wanted his side in this activity. He was very grateful for full freedom of decision had left him. Especially since he bought his admiration during the reconstruction of Lisbon after the great earthquake of 1755, when the minister was too busy to think from the sale of the port. Marquis Rodrigo Barros, twenty-six, of medium build, olive complexion, dark hair and eyes blacks. He was very attractive although not possessing a distinct beauty. He had a gruff look even at a happier and more severe expression. "Senhor came a message for you!" His valet had delivered a letter sealed with purple wax on which was engraved the arms of Távora & Noronha. He had initially decided to leave it on the desk of his study and opened it quickly with the hope that it was not the usual invitations to dances or receptions during which he was bored to death. He turned toward the clock on the wall, five in the afternoon. He took an apple from the tray full of fruit lying on the table near the fireplace, and with great pleasure, had been drinking a nice glass of Porto rosé. That was the energy required to bear the thought of a boring party at the palace Freixo. The next evening he would have caused more than one drink before crossing the hall of mirrors and endure the tedious discussions of young noble women looking for husbands.

3.

She looked more at the large mirror in her room and she is no longer liked. She wore a cream-colored dress, which she put too much emphasis on his amber complexion. Her hair was pinned at the neck and some wavy locks fell over her shoulders. She had no desire to spend an entire evening with dancing and deafening chatter. Yet even she knew she had the right not to attend a social event. Her mother had just returned from Lisbon, where he had gone to visit his sister. "My dear you are very well Senhor Armando will be proud of you." The Baroness Carla Da Costa was a middle-aged woman still very fascinating. She had a beautiful light brown hair well cared for and the same olive skin of her daughter on which stood two large green eyes. "If you notice how I am dressed!" The mother was sitting on the bed and aviation took her hand. "My child, what's wrong?" The fear of hurting his parents had so much to push it even pretend to herself. In a moment he assumed an expression of joy, and with the lump in his throat, he smiled. "No, nothing. And that he might ultimately be too busy with his trade of gold and he is a bit tired." These modern men have so many financial interests to be followed to lose his head. However, it is a fortune for your future. Surely you will not miss anything." Just as she had feared their expectations were so rosy not be any question about the true feelings of his daughter. Perhaps it was also what happened to his parents too. He had never seen really happy and thought his future was to be a reply of that union. She was almost convinced to love the Marquis Silva.

Ultimately she could not be indifferent to his pleasant person. Doroteia was directed towards the door and she had a big breath before opening it and going to meet her fate unaware.

4.

Before going to the reception, Rodrigo was granted an hour in his barn, adjacent to the quarry the Porto to inspect his horses. He would have been happy with them instead of throwing in the confusion of the noble worldliness. He had put the first coat that had happened at hand without worrying about the mirror before going out in a hurry. Ultimately he was only fulfilling a tedious duty of society. The coach had accompanied him in the short journey along the Douro River, on whose waters the moon created the wonderful silvery reflections. When he arrived in front of the imposing building Freixo, he had been dazzled by the countless torches lit around the park and along the drive on the main entrance. Many were nobles who were preparing to pass through the large wooden door so that it was almost impossible to see the valets inspection staff of the calls. For his taste that promised little good crowd and already struggling to think of how many threads should have taken part. The driver had helped him to get out and waited his greeting before resuming his way home. He walked the few feet that separated him entry he regretted not being left in his stall in the company of his dearest friends, his three stallions. The hall of mirrors was really fascinating, could not deny that work of art that delight the eye of him who also did not like the architecture. The upper balustrade, built in the style of opera was full of people who watched the arrival of guests. Fortunately the music was low and very nice. After greeting the hosts had set apart to the large window overlooking the park while enjoying a glass of white port. "You should dance with me, instead of to stand there secluded and sad as a stupid spoiled child!" He turned abruptly and he saw a man from behind who was talking to a superior young woman sitting in front of him. "Good evening Marquis Rodrigo Barros pleasure seeing you again after so long." Armando Silva was peering with him suspiciously because he noticed his curiosity about his bride. "The pleasure is all mine. How are you?" "Very well. Can I introduce my girlfriend, the Baroness Doroteia Da Costa?" The girl was blushing in letting kiss her hand. Her large dark eyes expressed a great sadness. "Come on dear?" A decision had helped to raise aviation dragged towards the center of the room. She would never forget his last look before leaving the chair.

5.

She looked at him again before she starts dancing with Armando. she wanted to satisfy herself that she was not dreaming. As soon as she met his eyes he felt a jolt to the heart and then silence. As if the beating had stopped in astonishment of emotion so strong and new. If she could follow her instinct, she would have thrown his arms now. He looked after her and this had given to Doroteia the vague hope that he too had felt the same thing. He had a sullen expression but his eyes seemed full of sweetness. What was he doing? Where did she live? Because he had never seen before? Was he married? "Marquis Who's that?" "He is a crazy set with the production of Porto and care of horses. A man who bothers to do duels and ends very easily!" He had given the description all in one breath and then he looked at her straight in the eye as to analyze the reaction. Something told her that it was the rage to make him talk like that. She would not believe him. Her fear of being judged had again silenced, as if she half happiness. In her heart she was bored, but especially disturbed. Ever since the eyes of the Marquis Rodrigo Barros.

6.

He thought about her during the walk back to the store, but he had been banished that thought. He had no sympathy for Armando Silva and the curiosity about his future wife could only get him into trouble. And recently he had too many headaches. It was not easy to manage a winery just trying to realize the dream of a lifetime. So every other thought I had to stay outside. "Good evening Rodrigo. Did you enjoy it?" The Marquis Pombal was waiting in the lounge of the company. "Let's say I have not that much bored. What prompted you to Porto in the night? "I came to check the progress of the Society of General agriculture vineyards of the Douro. We must continue to safeguard the producers of Portuguese wine. I love seeing all these English who take the credit for our product!" "You can not fail to recognize that if they had not started trading this wine has never reached such a high level of quality."

"Exactly! Why be controlled at home? From tomorrow I intend to retest all trades made last year by not losing our main economic resource." Rodrigo sat on comfortable leather sofa and had a coat lying on the desk. He did not want to think about what would be expected tomorrow. When the marquis put something in his head did not give peace until realization. Therefore those who were at his side he was fully involved. He accepted a glass of Porto that the waiter was showing. If he thinks back to what he had been drinking until then, his head felt heavy and the urge to sleep took over. "Have you found the home for you?" "Honestly I have not sought. I was too busy with business to not have a free minute. "If you want, my dear Marquis Barros, tomorrow I can show you a beautiful palace that overlooks the Douro." Thinking it was just what he wanted. He was tired of sleeping in damp that office, where he spent most of her days. "Perfect. At least I can settle once and for all in this wonderful city!" He got up and he reached his desk to resume his coat. "I greet you. I feel that it's bedtime. Tomorrow I'll be honored to visit this building and if it is really interesting as I have said, I will soon define the purchase."

7.

"What a terrible headache." Doroteia was looking in the mirror while the Barones Alcira Delgado was combing her long hair curly. "Have you drunk too much last night?" "What are you saying? You know I almost never drink and if I do and to please the Marquis Silva or my father." But since he discovered that Rodrigo Barros would have gladly traded the Porto also tasted a barrel. He never rested that night. The man had bewitched and intrigued at the same time. In rethinking just felt a lump in my throat and felt an inexplicable desire to cry. He did not know what they were a mixture of feelings but took her breath away. As soon as she woke up she immediately thought about what to invent for him again. "Do you know that I heard last night that the company Barros Porto is very good and popular. I would like to make a gift to my father. Why not accompany me to the quarry to buy a box?" Even more strange was the fact that he could not reveal these feelings to his very best friend. The Baroness Alzira Delgado was his same age and she lived in the building from an early age. She was of medium height, blue eyes, brown hair and a translucent complexion. They shared the joys and sorrows together. Perhaps the dream of a love which until then had never arrived. "As you wish! You have a headache this morning but you're very generous. " "Yes. It 's not so much that I make a gift to my father and I think if you deserve it! Alzira put the comb on the marble vanity and she sat on the big four-poster bed. "It has brought you a fine husband, and very powerful and rich!" How could reveal his inner torment? Until now it had closely guarded, convinced that he would never understand anyone. Who could understand his misery if he was destined to a life full of ease and riches Marquise? "Indeed. It's true. So I call the driver arriving at this warehouse. " In her heart he knew that Armando only see those bottles in Porto would have been furious. But her instincts had taken that decision and she would never came back.

8.

Rodrigo had already checked all the barrels in the slot and gave the note to the young man in charge because they draw up a careful list." Tell my servant to prepare the coach to reach the Marquis of Pombal. As soon as the boy had turned to run his order he had seen two young noblewomen enter. He immediately recognized that she wore a simple white dress. The wife of the Marquis Silva! Dismayed had approached and bowed politely had to receive two unexpected guests. "Hello, can I help?" "Hello, I am Doroteia Da Costa. We met yesterday evening during the reception at the Palazzo Freixo. I heard that you make a good port and I was curious to taste it to decide whether to give it to my father." He had watched her closely and noticed a redness due to an obvious embarrassment. Surely it was not easy for a woman present in a cave without any male support. "Come, sit down! I offer you some cake before tasting my wine? I don't think that it is not indicated for a young noble women drink alcohol without having first eat something!" He had made into his study and after they were sitting on the big leather sofa, the waiter had placed on the small coffee table a large silver tray filled with butter cookies. "Thank you for your hospitality. Not to sound rude in being forgotten to introduce my friend. Baroness Alcira Delgado who had the kindness to accompany me. " The girl, with delicate features and diaphanous, smiled shyly. "Very honored to meet you" "The honor is mine Marquis Barros. I heard about you. But if I have to be more sincere lover of horses not for your wine." He was laughed for the frank sincerity of that lady. High society now everyone knows to be very gruff and reserved. Often before going to a dance or a boring reception spent hours in his stables to look after and ride his beloved stallions. Nothing made him happier than those moments. "I must admit that it's true! The company of a horse is often greater than that of a person or at least has the security of never being judged!" Doroteia seemed at ease. He looked around and, often, arranging the folds of silk. Her eyes looked sad and lost behind other thoughts. "Will you come to visit the quarry?" He had motioned to follow them and when they entered the large room where they were lying all the barrels of port, the two girls were left speechless. Then he gave them two large crystal goblets and had paid the rose. "I must admit that it is very pleasant and it has a very delicate flavor. Da Costa was the Baroness, smiling. "I want a whole case!" For the first time that timid girl had said something decisive and secure. Yet his eyes were always sad and absorbed. That look made him curious, but at the same time frightened him. Could not forget that she would become the wife of the powerful Marquis Silva.

9.

She left the quarry in a panic. Primarily thought of how he would react Armando to the sight of that coffin of Porto Barros. This idea was frightened, but not like her mood when he crossed eyes Rodrigo. She felt stripped of that look and she immediately felt her heart would never have loved no other man. I don't know, but already knew that he would never forget. You look a bit strange Doroteia. Is there something wrong? "They just lift carriage and had turned to the window without a word. "Nothing. Why do you ask? " "I saw you upset before the Marquis Barros. "No... Not that I know. Perhaps his character so elusive makes me uncomfortable." Alzira looked at her and then she smiled sweetly." Or maybe his being so surly that he struck to the heart!" She was knocked over by the observation of his friend. It was so obvious? She did not know whether to admit his weakness or hide it tenaciously. She had never lied to Alzira and did not seem right to do so even in this circumstance. Did not reveal the secret to this tender Armando Silva. "Let's say that I remained indifferent. But it's all forgotten... We speak of other things. Please! "Inexplicably felt fit to tears. "Doroteia love is always a nice feeling. We should thank God that allows us to try this wonderful feeling! "Now her cheeks streaked with tears. Do not want to be seen and kept her head turned toward the street. However he knew that his voice would betray his state of mind. "It's a feeling that I can’t afford. In two months I'm getting married! "

Porto, june 1757

1.

"Senhor Barros, what do you want to eat tonight?" Dolores, the old maid, standing in the middle of the great frescoed room, waiting patiently for his answer. "Cook whatever you like. I have no preference " She bowed and she left him alone. He took his bottle of Porto and, having paid a bit in his crystal glass, he looked out to see her two new horses grazing in the meadow adjacent to the park lawn. He bought the luxurious home only for his large stables. Every morning he spent a few hours riding and then he headed in stock. The work continued to give him great satisfaction and could enjoy the results tasted his beloved solitude of space. He no longer attend any reception unless they were accompanied by the Marquis Pombal. In that case he could not refuse any invitation and had to accompany him everywhere. He was too grateful for the trust that you can contradict. The sumptuous villa did not reflect his way of life but had bought for his foothold in the city so he can get up close his business. The sky was suddenly darkened and within seconds a pouring rain had fallen on the windows. Just like two months ago when he met the Baroness Da Costa. She was walking along the Douro with the same look sad and melancholy. She greeted him with a warm smile and she lowered her eyes on the road. He wanted to stop, but he did not have the courage. The Marquis Pombal invited him a few months before to the marriage of the young woman with Armando Silva, but in that case he had refused arguing a trivial physical ailment. He still could not explain the reason for that behavior, was only the certainty that he was sorry. Her sad expression had intrigued. Was not happy with her marriage?

2.

She had not married yet, because Armando had to urgently reach Brazil for some unfinished business. So they postponed the wedding at a date still uncertain. In those months she had not even had the time nor the desire, to ask if she was really in love with the Marquis Silva. Thinking about the marriage of their parents she believed the normal type of relationship had developed between them. She knew that Armando loved her, but he never did anything to show her affection. Like his father, he always managed to emphasize only her negative aspects. He knew her tastes and passions but not attempting to conform. She was believed that if the marriage of his parents had lasted so long meant that love should perhaps be. When he started, Doroteia refused to follow him, she had not felt like. Not to give further explanations, of which perhaps not even she knew the real answer, she cited the banal excuse of fear of the sea. Lately she also shrank the company of her dear friend Alzira. She did not know what to answer when asked why so much of his air of melancholy. She thought so, but she not found a proper answer to her malaise. Until that day in June, she not reviewed the Marquis Barros on the street. As if by magic, in a moment, she understood everything.

3.

"Senhor, run. Finally, the foal is born!" Rodrigo was raised in a hurry. He slipped the silk dressing gown and, in trying garments, he checked in the big time clock attached to the wall. The four in the morning. Rosabella decided to give birth at night. His happiness was so great to be able to dress in less than five minutes. He awaited for a long time this event and he did not want to miss even a moment of new life that foal. The vet was monitoring the mare while trying to get out of the little hay. He spent two hours in the stables. The time had passed so quickly when they don't feel tired. When he reached the back room, he collapsed exhausted on the big bed. The old maid, Dolores, had awakened at ten. After knocking several times on the door, received no reply, he had gently shaken. "Excuse me senhor but I thought you were ill! You never answered my calls. I'm worried and I came!" "Oh. What time is it?" He looked at the wall and stood up in a flash. "It 's very late! We hope that the Marquis Pombal not otherwise come to the warehouse will be trouble for me!" He hastily ate some butter cookies and he drank hot tea before getting into the cab and ordered the driver to go as quickly as possible. To her surprise at the entrance he noticed a car with the emblem of Tavora & Noronha. Two young boys were unloading barrels from a boat on the Douro. "Hi Marquis Barros. There is a young lady in your office who asked for you?" Curious he went directly into the large room at times when he placed his desk and two large leather sofas in front of the imposing marble fireplace. The young Doroteia was standing beside the large window overlooking the River. He had not noticed him because you were reading some ancient documents hanging on the wall. "Hello Madame Silva" The girl was startled and she was spun around. Her cheeks were flushed suddenly. Then he looked straight in the eye and she firmly replied to his greeting. "Hello Senhor Barros. I'd rather be called Da Costa if you please! "For the first time since he had met his gaze seemed safer and less melancholy. 'I think now you become the beloved wife of Armando. And then... " "No! We postponed the wedding because of work commitments are new arrivals. So I would like to be called by my real name, if there be trouble! "He would not insist that the sign had to sit down and asked the waiter to bring the Porto and pastries. "What brings you in my store? You must make a new present? "He was slowly sipping wine and looking around curiously. "We say yes... Then I heard one of your kids tell you that this night is born a colt ... and I wanted to ask if you could let me see. Here I am... I love the horses!" She pronounced the sentence as a long prayer with which he could not remember the words.

Her difficulty in having done was evident. It was an effort that the effort had cost her shyness view. Had softened to the point of even forgetting all daily work duties. After all the morning had started late, it would recover this time, happily lost, with early rising the next day. Doroteia stared at his hands twitching nervously on the folds of her simple dress peach. Rodrigo stood up and called the driver. "Prepare the carriage that I urgently need to get back to my stables and helped the Baroness From Coast to climb it!" She got up and he laid his cup of Porto on the coffee table. Before turning herself, she looked him. In those eyes he read an infinite tenderness and perhaps even gratitude for agreeing to her dear desire.

4.

She could not explain what led her to ask a favor so unscrupulous. A young girl praying in a marquis to bring her home to see his horses. He could have easily misinterpreted, but the die was cast. And for the first time in her monotonous life, she acted instinctively. The man inspired confidence but also a great curiosity. When she had seen, after all this time, too long, she felt a strong urge to hug him. She was initially ashamed of herself and she tried to close in silence the strange feeling. Then, a cool head, she realized he could not live a life of regret at not having known him more deeply. What better time if not now that the Marquis Silva was in Brazil? Course should have silenced his cheek to his parents, careful only to rumors and blind people to misery after their only daughter. During the short ride in a carriage they had not exchanged many words. The embarrassment of both was clear. Rodrigo looked out the window and seemed absorbed in thought. That silence troubled her more than any embarrassing question. He had a sigh and then, without thinking, she opened her mouth. "How you live in this house?" "Since the Marquis Pombal did to me this proposal. I immediately fell in love for the big stables where I could put all my beloved horses! "They were slowly approaching the palace. It was large and simple in style but also very nice. He had two great towers decorated with stone and the lower part covered with colored tiles. The famous Portuguese azulejos. A large dark wooden door stood at the center of the structure. The driveway was very tidy and clean the garden was immense and so green that it seemed almost fake. The car was traveling up the steep access Doroteia while admiring the beautiful views of the Douro, almost more breathtaking than the building where she lived since childhood. Arrived in front of the stables were down with the help of the coachman, and some young boys had joined them to welcome them." This is the Baroness Da Costa who came to visit the new born!" He had her his arm to lead inside a box, where a stained brown and white mare was heating a small bundle of his own color. As soon as they heard the footsteps of their master had risen to receive both. The foal could barely stand. He was so embarrassed by her tender and me want to hug him. But he could not afford such a gesture toward an animal that was not his. "You like it? Think that was born a few hours ago. It 'was really a wonderful feeling!" "Oh, I would give anything to have a horse of my own but my parents never wanted to agree to my request." Again he could not understand why he decided to talk about something so intimate to Marquis. The only response was to ask questions but do not go according to his instinct. What until now had never done. Only live to other people happy. Her parents, husband, relatives, noble ... But no one had ever asked if she was really happy! At that time could claim to have tasted at least the thoughtlessness of something new. Something that she had chosen for himself if... Not always guided by others. "You are far more solar today. Your expression has finally given way to melancholy smile." Were heading towards the great balustrade overlooking the

River Douro. The cool ocean breeze tousled the hair simple, humble ponytail. He was trying to reclaim it to take time to answer that question, in its spontaneity, had fully hit the mark. How could he lie? What should have been invented to justify that his happiness as opposed to his normal sadness? She sat on a stone bench and had turned his gaze to his beloved river. "And I feel a bit' misunderstood... It 's hard to say, but my parents have great respect for me and impose their will on every decision of my life!" Now she was really naked. As if she had finally found the opportunity to get rid of a burden. Even if only in words. "It can happen. Sometimes parents act for our own good and end up, paradoxically, by pushing toward the raw misery! But I think that the Marquis Silva can appreciate and take adequately cares for you "Here this was precisely the point. Nor had he ever understood or at least made to feel appropriate to situations. Opened his mouth only to criticize or to say what to do, who should attend and even what to think of the people. "We say that sometimes you forget even my presence. But this can be excused ... With all thoughts of work he has in his head! "He uttered those words sarcastically and had immediately regretted it. To try to defuse the situation had a big smile. "Sometimes we men are a bit 'careless'" Indeed... But tell me you are happy with your work? "The Marquis looked at her, then he turned toward the stables. "I love my job and I am proud because it also allows me to devote myself to what I love most: my horses!" When she crossed her eyes she felt a sense of infinite tenderness. Unable to read the passion for these animals so fascinating. "I envy you. I too wanted to create something of my hand and I always left overwhelmed by the duties to others. So I ended up silencing my most intimate desires! "He sat beside her. The place had not had too much away. Strangely, the man inspired more confidence. "It's never too late. You must believe in yourself and try to achieve whatever you care about. Start by thinking about what you value most and try to implement it. " He looked away from her pretty face and was staring at the grass at his feet. Without thinking he had uttered the phrase that experience a ringing in her head since the beginning of that wonderful day. "One thing dear to me I've already done it! To come to you... Since I first saw you, I have not forgotten! "

5.

After he having seen her in the warehouse, where the coach of the Tavora & Noronha was waiting for her, she returned to home. The audacity of that girl left him stunned. He was surprised by her reckless honesty in contrast with her character always so shy and taciturn. He didn't know what was the real Doroteia. But this revelation driven to see her in a different light. She was bound to one of the most powerful men in Porto and he had not allowed to enjoy her delicate beauty, both physically and mentally. Before she let go, he was trying to kiss her but he could not afford a misstep. He could think that he took advantage of his unexpected declaration. It was not a gentlemanly behavior. Despite everything he was already thinking about how it can be reunited. The horses could be the best excuse to invite her back into his home. What would have happened after that could neither imagine nor planned? He could not forget that she was still another woman. The Marquis Silva would not allow to Doroteia even to greet him in public. Hatred against Rodrigo was more than evident, although unwarranted. They never had what to talk about something, but not what clash. After he got out of his carriage, he was directed back to the barn to check the handsome colt. He was sleeping peacefully beside his mother. If he had seen Doroteia, she would definitely moved.

6.

She could not sleep. Or rather she could not think of the Marquis Barros. She knew that she was open with her bold statement but had not been strong enough to control herself. She absolutely no thought to the consequences of that gesture. Now she wondered how she should act. Her heart made her want to see again as the reason he repeated that he was only doing a disservice to itself and to Armando. She could not hide behind a feeling of friendship because he knew he was not and never would be state. "Doroteia, do you awake?" Alzira's voice seemed agitated. She had got up hastily out of bed and had hurriedly through the parlor to reach the door to his apartment. The girl was waiting with a worried face. "Hello! But what happened to you that two days while living in the same building can not I meet you? "Doroteia had worked his way up to his room and began to dress while her friend sat in the chair at the bottom of the bed. "I felt unwell. Lately I have severe headaches that make me sleep badly and so many forces do not have to face the day! "He gives that stupid lie looking in the mirror does not meet the eyes of Alzira. "But if I came several times to knock on your door and you never responded!" "You see I was trying to rest and I have not heard." "Not you... but yesterday your waitress came to the door and told me not to I saw you all day!" Inadvertently the comb with which she was mending her hair had she fallen out of hand. A sign of nervousness that she tried to disguise and she collected on the fly. "Ah. Already I had forgotten to warn yesterday that the seamstress had to go downtown and then I spent more than they should... I'm sorry, but with this terrible headache I have not asked to accompany me because I was a little company!" She had bitten her lip higher the tension waiting for her response. "Let's say I pretend to believe. You know that you know very well and so long to understand that there is something you say. Do not insist!" Doroteia pretended not to understand and she stood up abruptly. "Let's go for a walk in the park? I need to relax a bit before it gets too hot. "

7.

"Senhor, no mail for you this morning. I'm sorry." Armando was controlling a large amount in his study for accounting some papers. The waiter left a cup of tea and biscuits before leaving again to his work. Days that were not received news from Doroteia. He didn't know what to think. If something had happened to her future in-laws would have surely felt. So what could go through her head? He had no idea what to think. He never understood why she felt so far away when they lack and when the next was not able to express his feelings. Certainly the cold behavior of the girl was not so inviting. It was not a correct explanation, but he knew that a little 'influence that his gruff and aloof behavior. Yet now more than this the days passed the darkened silence his increasingly unable even to work with due concentration. "Senhor, sorry but you just get a letter for you from Portugal. Perhaps this is what you expected! "His servant was entered into the study without knocking, was still out of breath for the long run. "With Miguel, you can leave it on the desk. As soon as I finish this review will read the statement. " The boy looked at him puzzled. Will certainly have thought that these nobles are really strange, so want one thing and then get it when they lose all interest. Armando did not even look up from the paper which he was correcting. He would not show his excitement for finally received the long awaited letter from Doroteia. Only when Miguel had closed the door behind him, he thrown the stylus from one side of the table, his hands still stained with ink had torn the envelope.

Porto, June 1757

My dear Armand,

I hope that your work will follow smoothly.

My life quietly awaiting your return.

With love

Doroteia

If he had waited so long this letter should recognize that he was disappointed. Two lines showed a somewhat formal and too far behind the woman who this year was to become his wife. Reason told him to forget every bad thought. The heart invited him to return to Portugal soon as possible.

8.

In less than a few minutes she found herself at the gate of the villa of the Marquis Barros. She could not resist from going to see him. In her heart she knew that her passion for horses was only a trivial excuse. She needed to see him again, she had to figure out if what she felt for him was just her imagination or true feeling. She had done nothing but think in the last two days. While crossed the great gate access saw the silhouette of Rodrigo in the distance. She was almost sank when she crossed her eyes. He always had that look of surly that intrigued and attracted at the same time. Only needed a moment to transform it into a wonderful smile, just like he was doing at that time to accept it. "What good wind brought you into my house this morning?" She was dropped from the carriage in a hurry without even greeting the coachman. "I wanted to see the colt... and you..." She uttered this sentence with the blush on the cheeks but she felt the need. Bewitched the man more than any other human being on earth. When he was before him forget everything else and the world seemed to be only joy. "I'm happy because I felt the need to see you!" Hearing those words Doroteia experienced the sensation of floating in the air she was so much happiness that it had originated. It was left to lead the hand towards the stables. Although the route was held in complete silence, he felt so close to his rider by being able to imagine his thoughts. They had visited the little colt who began to make his first tentative steps. She stroked him and she admired the Marquis who had to take care of the mother. After they had sat on the bench stone from which one could admire the Douro. "I am honored by your presence... and I must say also in difficulty! Envy Senhor Armando Silva for his fortune in able to marry! "Doroteia fixed his gaze toward the river because she was too much happiness to hear those words. It meant that Rodrigo had a minimal interest in her. And even if it created many problems in the joy of feeling was reciprocated too big. She felt his hands on his shoulders to lie down, then he sits down beside her. "I dreamed of being able to change my future. Or better to have the opportunity to choose a life to live in my heart and my thoughts! " "And you think you can do it? "I looked at by decision and he took my hand gently. "You would be the best decision to be taken!" Rodrigo smiled tenderly and gently he lowered it was to her, kissed her passionately. Doroteia had returned just as daring. Such was the desire to stay in each other's arms can not even to pull their lips. The sound of a galloping horse brings them sharply to reality. "Senhor your groom asks for you" The boy stood motioning to follow. "I come immediately. Give me time to greet my guest! "Fortunately it had softened the embarrassment that was created after the unexpected kiss. "Be not uneasy to accompany the coach. I beg you. Are already in trouble enough for what just happened! "Rodrigo had bowed and kissed her hand. "Until we meet again I think any time of day and night."

9.

After sending twelve boxes he brought to England by one of his most loyal customers, Rodrigo got up from his desk and he reached the warehouse. When he was confusedin his ideas all those barrels arranged in line reassured him. It was his greatest pride. His dream had come true against all odds. But even that harmonious vision reassured him about his feelings. That girl, Doroteia, put him in confusion. The same situation was not easy. She was destined for a wealthy and influential man. As for trying to take her off from his mind he could not do it. He thought about how their story would have been if there had Armando Silva's shadow looming on their hypothetical happiness. Maybe it was the impossibility of having to make her want her more. He didn't want to think about it, but he just wanted to see her again as soon as possible. A quick look at the clock he realized that they were already late for his daily ride. An attractive ride astride his stallion would preferred to forget for a few hours these damned heart problems. If they could define problems...

10.

"I searched you all day. Where were over?" The Baroness Carla Da Costa was seriously looking down her daughter. Doroteia tried to hide the apparent embarrassment combing long brown hair. Her hands were trembling for fear of betraying her sweet secret. "I went for a healthy walk in downtown. I see nothing wrong!" "I hope it really well but it did not convince me that much. Have you ever spent whole days on the books in the library or in the park watching the Douro together in Alzira. Instead, lately it seems that you have forgotten even your closest friend." She knew that this was her biggest flaw and she had to do something to get help from Alzira to hide her burgeoning romance, because Doroteia knew that this was the true love, what twists life, what makes you dream and often does not sleep." "I wanted not to disturb. Not much love going downtown. But tomorrow I will ask for a walk." The mother continued to stare skeptical and thoughtful. Before opening the door she turned and she looked warner, then she had launched a last arrow. "See that you do not forget also the Marquis Silva!" Unfortunately she hit the mark...

11.

"What do we do here at night?" Rodrigo was about to cross the gate on his horse with the intention of reaching as his favorite tavern every evening. Doroteia just stepped from his carriage and she was watching him. "I wanted to see you and no intention of going to bed early. I would not sleep and I spent the whole night thinking, "That girl had courage because she was playing with something bigger than herself. Or perhaps not well aware of what he was doing. She stretched her arm and aviation helped mount a horse. Only when he heard his trembling hands wrapped around his waist was off at full gallop. He knew that lead to his villa was not a good idea and then decided to go on an ocean beach. The capes they wore both ensured a bit 'of anonymity. The cool air of evening unleashed his face and gave him no time to think about how to act. His heart was giving a joy never experienced before, and decided to eat it without thinking about the rest. Comes closest to the coast as the streets were deserted. After half an hour trotting had stopped in a small sandlot and had tied his horse to a tree. "Please, will you follow me?" "Where are we?" He closed his eyes with his hands, whispered in his ear. "Try and breathe the smell of this air and noise in the distance. There will be difficult to understand." She brought her hands to her mouth and with a joyful voice she exclaimed: "Oh but we are at sea! What I always dreamed of a beautiful beach at night! "Just let her enjoy the scenery she embraced him with enthusiasm. "Hey... Remember we are always near Porto .. Come let's go for a walk on the beach. I have a flashlight with me! "We had set out hand in hand in silence. Occasionally Doroteia lifted the skirt of her dress in green silk to walk more comfortably on the sand. Rodrigo looked at her and he smiled. Gently he stroked her cheek and he kissed her on the head. He closed his eyes and always aspired to do the pleasant smell of her skin. Then he sat on the sand. Before doing so he stretched out his cloak to avoid the humidity of the sand. "What have you invented to go out at night?" "Nothing ... I just fled. I do not think anyone is looking for me in the room. Or at least I hope so! "He looked down on the sand and had passed his arms around his legs. The only idea that could find all felt mounting anxiety. His last wish was to find himself challenged to a duel by the Marquis Silva. Had his arm around her shoulders and left it laid his head on his chest. The scent of her long brown hair the intoxicated. "Today I thought that if you had not promised to another, so I would like to have you by my side for the rest of my life." When Doroteia looked up at him, kissed her with transportation. They were lying on the sand and had been embraced in silence for long minutes. "I would love to have you met before. Yet I still have the mad conviction that they could change course of my destiny. " Rodrigo began staring at the sky. There were millions of shining stars accompanied by the impetuous sound of the sea. "We were all against. Your parents, all the nobility of the Portuguese... we would be considered crazy" "Crazy, but in love and so happy." How naive was that girl. Maybe she had all the courage of which he felt lacking. He was so good in his company but the price to be paid to state his feelings seemed too high. Activity had to efendi him. "Know that whatever you decide I'll be waiting here." He kissed her again and she untied the satin ribbon that bound the rebellious hair. "I can't live without you. Your smell accompanies me every minute of my day and at night I sleep poisons. All of a sudden became pensive and stood up abruptly. "What?" "I think you need to see me in front of your gate or the driver will go my way not seeing me again!" She began to shake the beautiful green robe and she had re-tied hair ruffled by the soft sea breeze. "As you wish. You should not experience further problems. Let's go now!" Rodrigo was done seriously, he taken up the mantle and he walked to his thoroughbred. While helping to get Doroteia she looked at him and gently kissed him on the forehead. "You are the joy of my life. I will do everything to have you by my side forever."

12.

She returned silently to her apartment, but, as soon as she cross the main entrance of the palace, the music reminded her of the dance that Tavora & Noronha prepared for that evening. It was only eleven o'clock when she ran in the room could wear a dress in a hurry and go into the hall of mirrors. She had to think to invent an excuse by her parents that certainly they should be worried about not having yet seen. "I waited for your you!" Alzira was sitting on the velvet chair at the side of his door. "Hello. What are you doing here? "No. Now listen to me without so many stupid questions misleading. I told to your parents that you did not feel so good to help you, but I think that it's time that you're really honest with me!" There was no reason to continue with the farce was to tell the whole truth in hope of being understood. "Come in to talk about it while I try to change my dress. There is still time to introduce me to dance?" "Do you have to do otherwise I have no idea what to invent to hold off your anger." She brushed her hair and she was collected them in two long braids that formed a lovely bunch of flowers which had added fresh. While wearing a pretty yellow silk embroidered with precious pearls had told his furtive meetings with the Marquis Barros. I had tried not to make eye contact friend and hoping for your understanding. "Have you driven in a pickle!" Those words had made her shudder. "Why do you say that?" Alzira had risen and tied the tight corset. "Why do not you know the Marquis as Armando and in my opinion, you were a fool to trust him! Could tell everything and disgrace forever!" Doroteia had spun around almost in a panic to the sincerity of her friend. At the bottom she was so impulsive not think about the consequences of her act. She let herself be guided by her heart and she forgotten everything else. Alzira was putting the time before the harsh reality. She could look for other excuses. Rodrigo could recount what it happened between them, that she had confided to him and, worse, he could have exaggerated their intimacy. She almost fainted, an annoying cold sweat was pouring from her forehead. But he must not fall to the ground. Not at that time. She had to go to the ball to clear her continuing leaks from the company. She grabbed the fan lace on her bedside and only after having flown with apparent calm she started toward the door. Alzira followed her in silence. No, the Marquis Barros would never have dared to turn their backs. Although he loved her with the same intensity that she loved him. Yes, she was sure!

13.

"Good evening Marquis Silva what are you doing on this ship? You are already back in Portugal? "Armando turned suddenly and he found himself in front of the baron Carlos Carvalho, his old childhood friend. "What a nice surprise! How are you? For years we meet." They had embraced with enthusiasm and, after the usual questions of ritual, they sat on a wooden bench. The sea breeze was whipping their faces while sipping a glass of port served to them by a waiter, a young Brazilian boy. "What brought you to Brazil?" "I purchased a large ranch with a large plot of land. I decided to move there with my wife and my children!" "Not bad... then you have abandoned the idea of founding a winery? At the time the university seemed to think this dream come true!" "I love the port but I realized following the implementation phases of the Marquis Barros. And I realized that I had what he takes to follow that road!" The mere mention of the Marquis bothered him exceedingly. Yet he did nothing to try so much hatred towards him. And that anger was increased when he saw him who saw Doroteia with sweet eyes. No one could take away from the head she had a soft spot for him, was all too evident. And maybe even the fear of his approach had prompted him to shorten his stay in Brazil. For the first time he had put the work in the background. "Since do you know the Marquis Barros?" Carvalho supported the pair of doors on the wooden table before them and he accommodated the sleeves of his purple coat. "Since we were children. We played together throughout our childhood and then we gathered at the university. I followed every step of the founding of the winery's tiring." Armando did not know how to get more information without giving the impression of an annoying busybody. He must still take risks in order to have a better idea then how to act. "Even I know for some time but have never been able to clearly understand what it is. He seems very distant and reserved." "I must confess that it is not easy to be near him, because he is grumpy and overly introverted. But he is also sensitive and has a big heart and available even if wounded." "He would not seem so sorry!" "An older woman with whom he has had a troubled love affair has left him for another man. Then each time she returned to find him, he never pulled back. He trampled his pride in the hope of spending his life alongside this ungrateful woman who has always abandoned. I'm sure if she tried again to see him, he not be able to deny." "I understand... is not easy to give to the person you love. Yet I noticed that the power to attract many women to his side!" "Yes. Every time we went to some dance every girl did everything to show off. He had many stories but all short. No longer able to form a relationship lasting. Perhaps in hopes of her return. I hope you do not fit a woman so disreputable " He didn't know if you breathe a sigh of relief, or have even more fear. In the end, a wounded man is weaker!

The Hall of Mirrors was filled with guests. Alzira went sent to the big windows facing the garden while Doroteia followed her in silence. The mere thought of seeing her parents gave her goose bumps. She was afraid of their criticism for her continued absences. She didn't know if her good friend would give the necessary support. She seemed upset about her affair with Rodrigo, but sympathetic. "You're going through a bad time. Maybe you just afraid of the big step that you're addressing. Ultimately, marriage is not an event and then every day should be forever. I think this will have a bit mind clouded in confusion and put your heart!" Alzira was talking to her as she watched the couples who danced to the center of the room. "No! No... I am really in love with the Marquis Barros. I'm so well in his company. I feel that we made for each other. I can not imagine a future without him by my side. " "I hope that you're wrong and that he is not making fun of you!" Doroteia felt a jolt to the heart. Why was it so difficult for someone to accept the evidence of the feelings and look increasingly an obstacle to a hypothetical perfect love? "I have full confidence that you love me because I love him. Respect me and accept me for who I am. I never feel concerned as when I am with Armando. I'm just myself!" Alzira was about to reply when the Countess Amalia Da Mina had approached them with a glass of Porto rose in her hand. "Good afternoon, Baroness Da Costa, how are you? And it's long time to see." Actually she not looked her for more. She knew that she was in close friendship with Rodrigo and she did not want discovered their secret. But the smile that had sent nearly had experienced a slight sarcasm in her voice. Was he already knows his secret? The Marquis Barros told her something? "Lately I have not had much desire to attend the receptions. I felt a bit tired... " The came over to one ear, making sure Alzira not hear her, hiding her mouth had spoken with the range covered in feathers. "Perhaps you have attended other places more pleasant but more dangerous to the safety of your heart!" Doroteia was almost unconscious on the nearby red velvet chair. She spent her forehead damp, trying to hide the embarrassment, she mentioned her friend to leave them alone. The Countess Da Mina was accommodated at her side. "Do you feel bad?" No. Only a slight dizziness. I think that you will know my situation. Have you spoken with the Marquis Barros?" "I'll see almost every day. I promised to his mother that I would faithfully followed to make sure that everything was going well. We are friends of the family forever. And you know very well. And as if it were my son!" Amalia was a middle-aged woman, independent and lover of travel. In the past they were frequented often because united by their passion for reading. They were in the park of Tavora & Noronha and they read a few steps together and then they comment on it. She knew what she knew the family Barros, on purpose, had sought to avoid not reveal her affair with Rodrigo. But she had reckoned that he would certainly confided in her. The affection that bound them not allow secrets. Doroteia but was not very good at trying to find out more about her beloved knight, she could not investigate. "Be careful. I think you chose the wrong person. He is a wonderful boy, but very unstable. He can't keep a romance for over a week. I think his heart is still in the hands of the stupid woman who has repeatedly hurt! "He uttered the last words with so much anger by dropping her fan on earth. "I knew nothing. He never mentioned you. " Amalia took her hands in his and looked almost with pity. "When we are injured is not easy to accept reality. This lady, much older than him, he attended for a long time then he went with another man and back again. Rodrigo has always forgiven and never pulled back. I think if he came back again we would not think twice in accepting without considering all the pain that has caused "the Doroteia listened incredulously. He thought she would never hurt. I saw so sweet and affectionate they can not choose another man. His irritability hide his true nature, gentle and caring. "I did not know that she was so hurt. I do not ever given the impression. " "You know well but be careful to hide because its instability love can be very dangerous for you. Will never have the courage to confront the Marquis Silva, nor take their responsibilities for your story. He has nothing to lose. You lose your honor, but especially your heart! "

15.

"What do you say? You have not yet addressed your daughter? I can't believe to my ears. I knew that I should not trust the Marquis Barros. I never liked him!" Armando had just returned from Brazil and he was discussing with Baron Da Costa in his study. Doroteia had not yet informed of his arrival. Initially he wanted to surprise her, now, he just want to address her. What he found was destroying his heart. "We just knew. They meet in his home. I don't know what happened between them..." Armando was clenching his fists with so much strength to do almost bleeding hands. “Make her call! Please. Immediately! Damn it!" He threw a kick at a velvet chair that was overturned with a thud on the ground. "Calm down, otherwise I will have to call a palace guard. I don’t want a scandal arises or that the hurt. She is always my daughter!" Baroness Carla Da Costa was crying incessantly. She had not uttered the word, she continued to dry her tears with a handkerchief full of silk lace. She was lying on a couch staring into space. "Darling, I beg you please stop sobbing. Do not solve anything that way!" The waitress had deposited a tray of tea and some butter cookies. Armando was approached near the future mother-in-law and he offered her a steaming cup. "Drink at least able to calm. I do not want no confusion nor give out speeches poisoned. This absurd situation has made me realize how I tied to Doroteia. I swear that I will not give up so easily to your daughter!

16.

"Sorry Baroness Da Costa, but your mother and your father want to see you soon!" Doroteia was reading a book on the terrace of her apartment. The news made her jump up suddenly. She had a bad feeling but did not want to ask questions at the young waitress. "Okay. I'll be with them within ten minutes. Time to settle the hairstyle. As soon as she came out she looked at her reflection in the mirror. If her face conveyed her happiness had become physical half. She had lost weight without realizing it. She was consumed by the idea of discovery and trial. And now had come the fateful moment when she felt. She opened the door and with trembling hands, he walked in the long corridor painted, her legs felt heavy as stones. She had often imagined that time and she was believed to be able to easily overcome with a strong dose of courage. Now the push heroism seemed to run out into nothing, mysteriously vanished. If only she could meet Rodrigo first would find the necessary push to force her feelings. Young women with sumptuous clothes were traveling in the tea room for their afternoon meeting. Doroteia had always hated that stupid habit where every speech focused on life in the city. She preferred to go down in the park, sit on a stone bench and read a good book while watching the slow flowing waters of the River Douro. Often read romance novels and daydreaming. Wanted to be treated like a princess and not with the detachment and indifference that reserved the Marquis Silva. Armando seemed to be taken only by himself and incapable of giving affection. Now, after meeting Rodrigo, she was almost certain that he loved her and would never want as you wanted. One more reason to be strong and face the decision of her life. The footman to the side door of the apartment of the parents had been open just saw her coming. In enter the small corridor that led to the study of his father had tried to maintain an upright and secure. All her courage collapsed when, sitting in front of the fireplace, she had seen Armando. She was not dreaming:

he was himself, in flesh and blood. His expression was harsh and sad at the same time. He seemed almost ready to cry. His mother, however, was already sobbing like a child. The storm had already broken out. "What are you doing still standing there at the door? Enter now please! " His father had a harsh tone and strong. She had never seen him so angry. "Good evening. What happened? Armando're already back home? "While trying to hide her emotion her voice trembling. The Marquis Silva stood up suddenly and went up almost menacing face. "You also have the courage to ask some silly questions? I think you only have to meet... but damn what you believe he's back in Porto so fast? "Doroteia had shrunk and he felt his cheeks redden with shame is that anger. His mother sobbed louder and shook his head in disapproval. " The Marquis Silva is right. O God, what shame to think that my daughter meets an another man. I have so hurt. I thought you were serious and respectful, and instead you launched into the arms of a perfect stranger!" At that point she had felt hurt and humiliated. How could so pull dance of judgments without knowing anything. Who had put around certain speech? 'Who has put certain things in mind? " "Keep quiet. Your mother is right. I did so to find such a family friendly like Armando and you... You turn your back and I throw away all our effort to secure a future respectful." "Are you angry in vain because I do not know what you're referring to." Armando had a hit with empty cups that had shattered into a thousand pieces." Would you say that the name Rodrigo Barros does not tell you anything? What you believe to continue to pretend?" She felt a sinking heart and had almost seemed that he had stopped for a moment that seemed an eternity. "Well yes! I know Rodrigo very well and I am sure of his feelings towards me. He loves me and treats me like a queen!" The Baron Da Costa had risen suddenly and had thrown to the wind maps arranged on a work table. "Do not you dare talk like that. Not sure what you're doing. Into the arms of a notorious libertine who has never managed to have a serious and dignified history! Never let marry a man who will not give economic security to which I aspire!" She felt trapped but mostly misunderstood, abandoned by her parents. "Okay, do not ask you anything! I'll decide for myself, and I take the trouble to everyone. Who asked you for help or who gave you the right to plan my future? "Doroteia had not expected was a direct response and in tears toward the stables. She ran so strong that she could not even see where she was going. Her head was spinning and whirling hair were loose on her shoulders while some curls tickling her neck. She stumbled several times on her own dress while the groom reached that would have saddled one of the many Andalusian horses of the Tavora family & Noronha. She is meeting Rodrigo and she is telling everything...

17.

Rodrigo had not slept well and he was not able to do anything all day. The boy involved in the shipment of barrels of Porto was of little help. Every time in which he looked at the door of his office to ask advice on committees to evade his head was lost in the void. Rodrigo thought to Doroteia and what was nice to be with her. He had always been reluctant to think of getting married, but now he was sure that this girl, so sweet and sensitive, could share a happy future. This also his safety led him to think you can challenge to a duel while Marquis Silva to have his side forever. He stood up and he reached the window that looked out on the river Douro. A warm summer sun created beautiful reflections of silver on the water's edge. The quays were crowded with sailors intent to load barrels on boats direct port in England. He was so absorbed in his thoughts that he had heard a knock at his door. "Senhor, Baroness Da Costa calls for you!" Rodrigo turned and he sent a big smile to your servers. "Let it go now and offer some butter cookies with tea. Please! "Doroteia was burning her cheeks and her eyes swollen from crying. She just came threw herself into his arms. "Love what's going on? What have you done? Have a look so distraught! "She wore a pretty white dress that showed off her long brown hair. "Armando... My parents and Armando have found it!" Rodrigo was almost sank. Pretended security continues to hold her tight but she heard a piercing pang. He began to stroke her face and tears to dry. "Tell me what happened. Calmly. Sit on the couch, breathing slowly." She began to explain the unexpected arrival of the Marquis Silva and hasty accusations of parents and her firm decision to leave the palace and go live with him. Her hands trembled and his eyes facing the floor not to show his suffering. When the waiter had served a tray of cookies Doroteia had refused to eat , but she accepted a hot cup of English tea. "I knew that sooner or later someone would have shared. It was too good a feeling that we were living. But I will stay here waiting for you. Cost what my heart is in your hands! "I don't want to go back to the palace. I never want to see my parents. I hate that environment with all of myself. I was never so realized until I met you." He might not keep her. It would be a scandal that would put in serious danger of his pension winery. All Porto would speak of his inconsiderate and noble friends of Armando, most of the city, would never buy one bottle from him. "Listen, my love, you need strength and go home. Address this situation as best as possible. Now is not the appropriate time we are both tested by the situation." Doroteia got up and had thrown his arms like a child looking for love. She sobbed desperately. Among them was also the barrier of courtesy fall and had begun to give of yourself. Yet their effective symbiosis in behavior and feelings seemed to be enough to save the day. Rodrigo knew that he was not able to help. His character was not so strong to face such a test. He had held her and she tasted his scent. How to take forever with him...

18.

"Damn Alzira, but when do you arrive?" Armando continued to go up and down in the great palace park Tavora & Noronha. He sent a note to the closest friend of Doroteia to be able to talk as soon as possible. Perhaps she would help him understand what had really happened between his girlfriend and the odious Marquis Barros. He had never had a liking and now he understand because he was always seen as a possible rival in love. Exhausted, he decided to sit on a bench stone. His hands throbbed as he clenched his fists. He launched some porcelain trays on the door of his apartment, but the anger was not diminished. He felt insulted and overlooked by the woman he would marry in a few months. Perhaps he was not good to prove his love. Yes, because he was sure to love her, otherwise he could have sought the hand of any young nobleman of Porto. Every parent would be happy to have him as a son. His activities in Brazil gave him a high income, which together with his family possessions, made him one of the richest men in Portugal. "Good evening Senhor Silva. How are you? "Alzira was behind him and she smiled. She had her usual quiet and serene that loved Doroteia. In fact, whenever she spends time with her, she used to say: "With Alzira, I complete! She has the qualities that I love and I can never acquire. "Good evening, Baroness Delgado. I urgently need to see you and I guess you know very well why this is my calling." Armando turned to the Douro and he fists, clutching the stone balustrade with force. He was trying to dominate the raging anger that instead of diminishing, inflamed his soul. "I think you need some clarity. I will try to help you, although I have little to tell. I propose to take a walk in the park, not food silly talk about us." They started to walk and Alzira, without delay, told the Marquis Silva that she knew about the history between Doroteia and Rodrigo. Armando listened in silence. Not addressed pressing questions but simply looking around blankly. "Do you think that Doroteia love me? Or rather, who chooses not to marry again?" "I don’t know. I think that she is confusing... and..." "No. I can’t lose her. If you decide to go back, I'll be here waiting for her. And it’s unthinkable that after so great a disgrace, I may forget, yet it is the only solution to remain at his side." Alzira had stopped and she looked at him with a sweet and sympathetic air. "Then why do not you tell him? Why not have the courage of your feelings? I'm sure that she would love to know. No matter what she decides to do. You must be honest with her. I think what happened may be a new beginning for your future romance! Everything that happens, however painful it may seem it, is to face a trial and an opportunity to grasp!"

20.

Doroteia had just closed the door of her apartment, the maid had been informed that the Marquis Silva in the living room was waiting for her. The very idea made her sick and took away what little strength that remained. She could not refuse to see him, he was still her fiancé. She entered in silence in the room unannounced. Armando was sitting and he was holding his head with his hands. He looked so desperate. She had never seen shot down and almost defenseless! He stood up abruptly and he went to the meeting. "I've been waiting for. If you do not offend you I call you to break down the barriers that still exist between us." Instead of feeling compassion for the man who was making the first steps to conquer her really bothered her that behavior even more. "I see nothing wrong in giving you the... But I have no intention of listening to speeches sentimental coming-time expired. You've had months and months at your disposal to try to prove something to me but..." Armando had taken a hand of Doroteia and he viewed her with fresh eyes and appealing. “Please give me one last chance!"

EPILOGUE

When she returned to the home of the Marquis Barros, she was left speechless. The valet had announced that he no longer wanted to see her. Initially she was so desperate that she decided to join him in his vineyard and, fortunately, pride had turned away from doing so. She was questioned from the beginning by revealing her love as he had done nothing but wait for a future together that only she would win. "Remember that I'll be here waiting!" They were not words of a gentleman. Yet in the following days had passed several times in front of the stables and the house but never had the opportunity to see him. One morning, when she no longer hoped to hear from him, he had encountered on the street. He was riding while Doroteia was walking along the bank of the Douro. Few words were spoken without look at her. He continued to turn the reins in his hands. "It would never work! We were all against them and me with my job, I can't afford!" It was well served to just remind him that he had already be aware when he accepted the elusive history. At least he could have saved many promises compromising. She had not seen. Both avoided places unknown. She thought often but when she realized that love is not supported by courage is not love. Armando had remained at her side. She decided to give him his deserved chance. Even the joy of his parents, who as true bigots were worried not only to burst a scandal! That was his greatest disappointment. Understand that she was considered an object of exchange and a pawn to be moved according to their will. The only salvation was to leave her beloved city. She would never admired her Douro, the slow flow of water so that he could soothe. But it would benefit her health and, above all, her self-esteem. "Building a future together. Promise me you respect me and you treat me like a queen. Try not to raise his voice in front of other people and I do not overlook. A woman always needs attention. And the more interest you receive more affectionate to her man. Do not judge me for everything I do. I don't control. Please take me away from here. I don't want to live under continual review of my family! "Armando had remained silent then, after a big sigh, he looked Doroteia into her eyes. "Where'd you go?" Doroteia had a huge smile and started jumping like a child. "Take me to Siena! Please, the city has always been my dream ever since my father took me to watch a horse race. I never stopped thinking," He had embraced her and kissed her forehead. He knew that he could not hold back. Would have meant losing her trust forever. "And then, we are going to Siena!"

THE HOUSE FREIXO

The beautiful home of the family Tavora & Noronha, where stays Doroteia Da Costa and her family. The rear of the building overlooking the River Douro. It is currently under renovation to be turned into a Pousada of Portugal (old houses

converted into tourist facilities) If you want to stay there or just browse in this beautiful house:

http://www.pousadas.pt/historicalhotels/PT/pousadas/Portugal/Norte/PalaciodoFreixo/home/PalaciodoFreixoHOME.htm

Courtyard of the Palace

with a view over the Douro River.

The Hall of mirrors. Brought to light after the restoration that has made the Palace Freixo a luxury hotel.

View from one of the room of Palazzo Freixo.

Sebastião José de Carvalho e Melo, Marquis De Pombal, in a portrait of the painter Louis-Michel van Loo

PORTO WINE: Wine liqueur made exclusively from grapes from the Douro region, northern Portugal. In the photo of Quinta do Noval Port, the oldest company in Portugal, It has news of its existence in 1715. Date on which the family Rebell Valenta purchased the property by the same Marquis Pombal.

The Douro River that crossing Porto. On the background, the Ribeira, the oldest part of town and that defined by UNESCO World Heritage Site.

By a twist of fate this October (2009) I discovered that there really is a manufacturer under the name Porto Barros. Remains unchanged the words that there are no references to real people (except the Tavora family and the Marquis Pombal & Noronha) as the winery was founded in 1913 and is the most recent.

www.ingramcontent.com/pod-product-compliance
Ingram Content Group UK Ltd.
Pitfield, Milton Keynes, MK11 3LW, UK
UKHW020238250726
13967UKWH00001B/431